Until Death Do Us Part
A Chuck Polanksi Story

© Copyright 2024 / David Boyer / all rights reserved.
ALL Rights Reserved. This book contains material protected under International and Federal Copyright Laws and Treaties. Any unauthorized reprint or use of this material is prohibited. No part of this book may be reproduced or transmitted in any form or by any means, electronic or mechanical, including photocopying, recording, or by any information storage and retrieval system without express written permission.

Published in the United States of America by Lulu.com and Draft Digital 2.com

Until Death Do Us Part
A Chuck Polanksi Story

The true horror of existence is not the fear of death, but the fear of life. It is the fear of waking up each day to face the same struggles, the same disappointments, the same pain. It is the fear that nothing will ever change, that you are trapped in a cycle of suffering that you cannot escape.

And in that fear, there is a desperation, a longing for something, anything, to break the monotony, to bring meaning to the endless repetition of days.

1

Until death do us part.

I've always felt lucky for some unsuspecting, lonely, lady out there that we never met. That way, she didn't have to endure the torture of marrying a selfish, self destructive man like myself, and sit back to watch me make a mockery of my life.

Then again, who knows?

I might have found a woman that was just as intent on drinking herself into an early grave as I was, and we could have spent a short and not so sweet and blisssful life together.

But that's doubtful.

Most of the ladies from my generation had signed up for the long haul, in sickness and in health and all that good crap.

So, Chuck Polanksi, self admitted lush and aspiring writer, spent most of his useless life alone.

But, there were actually some decent perks to that lifestyle, too.

#

Such as, you ask?

Well, such as I was *single*, which meant I could stay up late and watch HBO and drink beer and smoke Lucky Strikes and eat leftover chili and fart and burp and be as lazy and gross as humanly possible, without offending anyone – and not that I would have given a damn, either.

Yeah, I know.

What's so special about the freedom to live such an abhorrent life style?

Nothing really. But then again, it's not really as much about the life style as it is the *freedom* to do so.

Give me my freedom and a bottle of single malt and my laptop any day, and I will show you a happy man.

#

Most days, anyway.

Like today, for example.

I was feeling just peachy, sitting at my laptop and typing away, when my cell phone rang, and when I looked at the screen, it was my onocologist's phone number.

My *cancer* doctor.

I let it ring almost ten times before I answered it. She said, "Are you sitting down?"

I said, "As a matter of fact, I am. So go ahead, spill the beans."

She said, "Your last PT scan didn't look so good, Chuck. I'm so sorry."

I said, "The lympnodes again, I presume?"

She said, "Yes, on the right side of your throat again, and the right lung."

I said, "Stage three?"

With a shaky voice, she said, "Yes."

I said, "Well, that's it then, isn't it?"

She said, "Not really. Why don't you come in to

my office in the morning, and we'll discuss it."

I said, "What is there to discuss? Stage three is a death sentence, right?"

She cleared her throat and said, "That depends on how you want to look at it. Postively or negatively."

I said, "What in the hell could be positive about stage three cancer?"

She said, "Please, just come to my office tomorrow and we'll talk about it, okay? I'd rather not discuss something this sensitive over the phone."

I said, "Fine, then. What time?"

She said, "Ten am too early?"

I said, "That's fine," and hung up. I'd heard enough bad news for one morning.

2

I had begun with a simple sore throat and a cough, with the cough being a bit more persistent than the soreness in my throat. In the past, these symptoms, for me, had been merely signs my sinus trouble was flaring up because of a change in the weather, so I simply purchased some over the counter medicine and thought no more of it.

A few weeks later, my cough had subsided, but my sore throat was becoming almost unbearable.

And how did I take care of my current affliction you ask?

Why, drinking myself into a stupor, of course. How else would a confirmed bachelor with an obvious death wish react?

Then again, at the same time, I didn't know it was cancer yet, either.

#

Then one night, as I stood in front of the bathroom mirror brushing my teeth, I saw it; a very small but visible lump under my tongue, and a small but visible lump on the right side of my throat.

I knew then that sinus trouble – or a bad hangover - was going to be the least of my worries in the future.

And so it goes.

#

Needless to say, the overall mood in the doctor's office the next morning was less than cheerful.

As I sat down in front of my doctor's desk, Kerry Pruett, a tall, slender, brunette with big brown eyes and a bright smile, said, "Well, Mr Polanski, I think we should discuss your options, first."

I said, "What's this Mr Polanski crap? Why is it doctors only use your formal name when conveying *bad* news?"

Forcing a smile, she said, "Fair enough. Chuck, I think you should consider radiation treatment before throwing in the towel, so to speak."

I said, "I thought you said my cancer is stage three. What good will more treatment do at this point?"

She said, "Maybe none, but we won't know until we try it first. But, there is something you should be aware of before you make up your mind. After all, you aren't at stage *four* yet."

I said, "That still doesn't sound very promising."

She said, "There are certain, possible side effects with the radiation."

Almost dreading to hear about it, I said, "Such as?"

She said, "Well, since your cancer originated inside of your mouth and spread into your throat, the radiation would have to concentrated in those areas. Which, at times, can result in loosening or cracking of the jaw bone, loss of teeth, and even deformity, which could be corrected with facial reconstruction."

I said, "So, in other words, my only options are

either to try the radiation treatment and possibly end up looking like a circus freak, or don't try it, and possibly shorten my life span even more."

Having to force that bright smile again, she said, "Well, yes, that about sums it up. I'm sorry, Chuck, really I am."

Standing to leave, I said, "Not as sorry as I am, I bet."

Then I walked out without uttering another word.

3

When I got home, I just sat at my kitchen table in silence for a few minutes, doing my best to gather my thoughts.

My mind racing and my heart pounding, I leaned back in my chair, closed my eyes, and took several deep breaths, exhaling, and opened my eyes.

Nope, I thought, glumly. *I'm not dead yet, still here to suffer some more.*

So I got drunk.

#

I'm not talking "buzzed" either.

When Chuck Polanksi decided to tie one on, go on a binge, he gave it one hundred percent.

When I first began my binge, I'd decided to sit down at my lap top and begin writing a brand *new* story, a story about a guy who had spent his life watching it fly by him like a blur, never have loved or felt love or had any luck but bad luck, and, as I sat there typing away, I sadly couldn't think of anyone more qualified than yours truly to pen such a sad tale of despair and loss.

So I typed away, and drank single malt.

#

About several hours into my new story, I'd realized that with each word I typed, each paragraph, each new chapter, my story was growing more depressing and hopeless by the minute.

With each twinge of inner pain, with each old memory revisited, I would take another drink.

And another.

And another.

By the time I was weaving back an forth in my chair and seeing double, well, that's all I remember – that is, until the next morning, when I woke up on the bathroom floor.

#

I woke up lying in a puddle of my own urine.

I had also busted my nose on the edge of the toilet, having apparently passed out again while voiding my stomach. My shirt was stained with blood, and my nose was swelled up like a balloon.

Looking at the sad image of a completely broken man in the bathroom mirror, I lowered down to my knees and began to cry, begging for death, because I knew even death had to be even better than this.

When I woke up again, my phone was ringing.

4

It was Kerry Pruett.

All I could manage to say was, "Yeah?"

She said, "Are you okay? You left in such a huff yesterday."

I cleared my throat and said, "Not really. Far from it, actually."

She said, "I'm sorry, Chuck."

I said, "Me, too."

She said, "Have you thought any more about the optional treatment? I don't mean to be pushy, but I need to know."

I said, weakly, "To be honest? I've been trying *not* to think about it. Can I get back to you?"

She said, "Sure. But don't take too long, okay? I'm worried about you."

I said, "I promise."

Then I hung up.

I had to void my stomach again.

#

After my sour stomach had finally subsided, I took a quick hot shower and dressed in clean clothes, and sat down at the laptop for another day of writing.

I'd skipped breakfast and opted for a cup of black

coffee {with a double shot of single malt just to steady my nerves} and I was on my way to another Pulitzer prize winning story.

I wish.

As I sipped my coffee and glanced up toward my living room window, I saw a moving van pull up out front, and back up to the building steps. I knew the only empty apartment in the building was Trish's old room, and I was of course very curious as to who would be taking her place.

Since her departure, that seemed like a lifetime ago now, I had considered that empty room as sort of a shrine to her, and her memory, and couldn't bear the thought of "just anybody" moving in there.

As I sat and watched the moving crew beginning to unload the van, I saw a small, blue, compact car pull up behind it, and a short, slender woman with gray hair and eyeglasses climbed out. She looked to be around my age, too, and I figured, hey, someone my own age to chat with, that's nice.

As she stepped closer, chatting with the moving crew, I could see she was very pretty, too. She reminded me of one of those library ladies. You know, timid, quiet, and looks like someone's grandmother – not that there was anything wrong with that, either. I was a member of the baby boomer generation, too.

Suddenly my day didn't seem so bad after all.

5

I sat there for a while, watching the pretty lady direct the crew with an iron hand but a friendly smile, until at last, the last cardboard box was unloaded.

The furniture – an odd but still tasteful mix of sixties, seventies and eighties décor, had already been unloaded, and taken upstairs.

As I watched the moving van pull away, I saw she still had several boxes to carry up the stairs, and, being the gentlemanly type, thought I'd offer to help.

As I walked out the front door, I almost ran right into her, and, starled, she almost dropped the box she was carrying, that read *fragile* on the top.

Feeling like a clumsy idiot, I said, "Oops! Sorry about that. I just wanted to help."

Cracking a friendly smile, she said, "Thanks anyway, but I think I can manage."

As she walked on by me, I said, "Are you sure? Some of those boxes look mighty heavy."

She stopped, turned back to me, and said, with a big smile, "Are you sure you can help? You almost knocked me down the first time you tried to make an impression on me."

Feeling more than slightly embarrassed, I said, "Was I that obvious?"

She said, jokingly, "Yes, but I thought it was

cute." She looked beyond me at the boxes and said, "Okay. Grab that one on the top if you want to."

So I did – and at the same time, became acquainted with Miss Catherine Sanders.

#

A few minutes later, as we unloaded the last two boxes on her living room floor, she said, "Do you drink coffee, Chuck? It's the least I could do after you helped me move those heavy boxes."

I said, "That would be great. Black, please, no cream or sugar."

She smiled and said, "Two black coffees, coming right up."

As she set about brewing the coffee, I sat down at the tiny kitchen table – that used to be Trish's table – and the letter I'd received from her long ago stuck out in my mind:

Dear Charles,

Yes, I referred to you by your real name. I thought it was only polite, and befitting, considering the circumstances.

I'm sorry I left in the middle of the night, like a coward, but I wasn't really sure if I could handle speaking to you face to face.

I never want you to think that I don't care about you at all; it's quite the opposite, actually. But, I didn't think I couild bear watching another father figure lose their pride, dignity, and maybe even their life to the curse of alcoholism.

I will always love you like a father, and never forget you, but for now, I must move on with my life, and for the sake of my son's life, too. I hope you understand.

I better sign off now. I'm waiting for a friend to pick me up and give me a ride to my new place.

I will always remember you, Charles, and someday, when you become a famous writer, which I have no doubt you will, I can buy one of your books, show it to my friends, and say, That's my Dad!

Take care, and be good.
Love and hugs,
Trish and Joey

By the time I'd finished reading it, I'd already shed a million tears and finished off half a bottle of single malt.

But that was *then*, and this is *now*.

A fresh start.

Catherine was back now, having a seat at the table and pouring our coffee. She said, "I hope you're not offended, because this remark stems from genuine concern, but you don't look so good. Have you been sick lately?"

Not wanting to tell her I had a hangover from hell, I simply said, "Well, I do feel like I've had a touch of the flu lately."

She grinned at me, sipped her coffee, and said, "What *brand* of flu, exactly?"

I said, "Come again?"

She said, "*Brand*, you know. Like beer or wine, or bourbon. What brand?"

I said, "Is it that obvious?"

She said, "Yes, I'm afraid so. I'm not trying to be judgmental, mind you. It was just an observation."

I leaned back in my chair, sipped my coffee, and said, "It's fine, no harm done."

She said, "I've been there, you know."

I said, "Been there?"

She sipped her coffee and said, "Where you are now. Feeling more than a little hopeless, drinking to escape it all. That's one reason I took early retirement from the library. I knew I couldn't handle it any longer."

I said, "Well, that's a strange coincidence."

She said, "What's that?"

I said, "When I first saw you outside, I wondered if you were a librarian."

She said, "Yes, that is *quite* the coincidence."

I said, "So, what happened, if I may ask?"

She said, "I'm a widow. My husband of twenty three years died a few years ago. Cancer, it was. Mercifully, he didn't suffer for long."

I said, "I'm so sorry. So, you used alcohol as a crutch, so to speak?"

She said, "Yes, and it almost cost me my reputation, and my life. But I went to AA meetings, got clean, and took early retirement. I've been sober now going on two years."

I said, "I wish I could say the same."

She said, "Want some friendly advice?"

I said, "Sure."

She said, "You have to *want* to stop, before it will work. When that day comes, you'll know it."

I said, "Thank you for the advice." I glanced at my wristwatch, and realized it was time to get back to work.

I said, "Well, I better get back at it. I'm working on a new story."

She smiled and said, "Wow...you're a writer?"

I said, "Aspiring writer, yes."

She said, "Could I read some of your work sometime? It would keep me from being so bored, too. I don't watch a lot of TV."

I said, "Sure. Why don't I drop some of my work off later this evening? I think it would be kind of neat to have a librarian critique my work."

She said, "It's a date, then? Say about seven?"

Standing to leave, I smiled and said, "Seven it is. Until then, Catherine."

"Until seven," she said, with a big smile, as I walked out. On the way downstairs, I was thinking, *I better take another shower.*

6

After taking a long hot shower and shave, I dressed in my best shirt and jeans {courtesy of Walmart} sat down at my computer table, and poured several three-finger shots of single malt whiskey – just to calm my nerves, you know?

As I sat at my laptop, it occurred to me that a former librarian might just enjoy some poetry, so I printed off a copy of the poem I'd published in a magazine several years before, to enlighten her as to my obvious, untapped talent.

Or, at least I *hoped* it would, anyway.

#

I arrived right on time – never keep a lady waiting.

Catherine answered the door in a long, flowing, beige sundress and open toed sandals. Her hair was tied back in a bun, accented by a hair clip shaped like a monarch butterfly. She couldn't have been more beautiful at that very moment – a moment I'd never forget.

She said, "Well, Chuck. Don't you look handsome tonight?"

I said, "And don't you look beautiful. What's the special occasion? I just dropped by to let you read one of my poems."

She said, "A lady doesn't need a special occasion to look good for herself, does she?"

I said, "This is true."

She said, "Well, come on in and sit down, I have some coffee brewing, and I can't wait to read your poetry."

As I took a seat at the table, I noticed that most of the boxes had been unpacked. I said, "Wow, I wish I moved that fast."

She smiled weakly and said, "Widows have to learn to fend for themselves."

I said, "Of course, I'm sorry."

She waved the remark off and said, "No worries. So, while the coffee is brewing, let me read your poem."

I pulled the printout from my pocket, unfolded it, and scooted it across the table to her. She picked it up, and began reading it out loud.

There are ghosts in my head
And a demon in my soul
My constant companions
The cancer cells now
I feel like I'm in hell
And it's so dark here

She stopped reading, and, blinking away a tear, she said, "Oh my God, Chuck. I had no idea."

I said, "Believe me, God had absolutely *nothing* to do with my life in the past. I've had no guardian angels watching out for me."

She said, sadly, "Are you referring to the cancer?"

I said, "I'm referring to my whole life in general, actually."

She said, "Are you sure that's not the alcohol

talking?"

I said, "Come again?"

She said, "I can smell it, Chuck. If you were wanting to keep it a secret, you should have chewed a stick of gum."

I don't know why I became so upset with her remark, but I suddenly felt so furious, and so angry with myself for not being able to stay sober for one evening, I flew off the handle.

I stood up, pushing my chair out behnd me so hard it flew across the room, and said, "I was nervous, excuse me for living."

She said, "Oh Chuck, I'm so *sorry*. Please don't be angry with me. I didn't mean anything by it."

I said, "Yeah, *sure* you didn't."

Then I turned and stormed out of her apartment, slamming the door behind me.

#

After sitting down at my laptop, and taking several deep breaths to calm down, I poured another three-finger shot of single malt and lit a cigarette. A man tends to do that when he can't even look in the mirror without hating himself.

Hatred and self loathing.

The two main components of my own sad personality – that is, if you could call it one.

But there was one thing for sure. I had just just stormed out on a very sweet lady, and even slammed the door in her face.

And now, I was going to feel sorry for myself, and get drunker than a barrel full of monkeys.

7

I woke up early the next morning, laying on the bathroom floor again.

I hadn't soiled myself this time, but I'd fallen hard on the linoleum flooring, and was covered with bruises and ached all over.

The life of a hateful, self loathing, drunk of a man, who intends, hell or high water, to drink himself into an early grave, before the cancer could do it for him.

As good an as excuse as any, I guess.

#

After voiding my guts of any impurities for the third time, I had attempted to eat some instant oatmeal, but it hadn't taken me long to realize it wasn't a good idea.

So, there I was again, before noon, sitting at my laptop, sipping single malt and typing away, as if I really believed there was anyone out there who would be even remotely interested in what I was writing.

Then, to add insult to injury, the big C hit me hard that day, making me feel weaker than ever, if that was even possible.

The side effects were the worst part of it all. The nausea and vomiting. The weakness and fatigue. The chemo pump they had surgically implanted in my chest, that looked and felt like I had a giant spider crawling around in there.

Oh yes...there were actually things worse than some day drinking.

Depending on how you would look at it, that is.

#

By the late afternoon, with nothing really being accomplished on my laptop, I'd retired from writing for the day, and had taken a seat on the front porch, in my old lawnchair, and sipped single malt and watched the sunset.

Indiana sunsets to me, were so peaceful and quiet and beautiful, helped me calm down, and took me back to the days when Trish and I and her son used to sit out there together and eat burgers and chat about our day and laugh at each other's corny jokes.

But those days were gone, and all I had left was myself and my bottle and my memories, my memory palace so full it felt as though my mind would literally burst at the seams.

As well as a sweet lady upstairs who probably thinks I'm a gigantic asshole.

And so it goes.

8

The next day, I woke up in my lawnchair, around daylight, with Catherine standing over me, with her hand on my shoulder, trying to wake me up.

As my bleary eyes focused on her lovely face, she was saying, "Chuck? Are you okay?"

Clearing my throat, I managed to say, "Do I *look* okay?"

She forced a smile and said, "Do you *really* want me to answer that question?"

I said, "Not really. What time is it, exactly?"

She glanced at her tiny wristwatch and said, "It's six-thirty-seven in the morning."

I said, "Too early to be awake, then."

She smiled and said, "In your current condtion, yes. Come on, let me help you inside."

#

Once she had helped me get situated on the couch, she had brewed some coffee for me and made some eggs and bacon on the side.

The very smell of the food made my stomach churn, but I knew I had to eat *something*, or I could end up in the hospital.

When the food was ready, she set the table and

said, "Breakfast is ready. I hope you can eat."

I sat up, half staggered my way into the kitchen, sat down, and said, "One question first."

Pouring the coffee, she said, "I'm listening."

I said, "Why are you being so nice to me, after last night?"

She sat down and said, "Why shouldn't I be nice? I knew it wasn't anything personal."

Attempting to swallow a bite of egg, I said, "You're right, it wasn't personal. And thank you."

She said, "For what?"

I said, "For being so understanding."

She said, "Well, I've been there, done that, remember? Who am I to judge?"

I said, "Yes, but then again, I'm an easy person to cast judgment upon. I almost beg for it."

She said, "That's nonsense. Chuck, would you do me a favor?"

I said, "That depends. I'm not feeling quite up to par today."

She said, "Would you tell me *your* story? I mean, how you became dependent on alcohol? I told you my story."

I thought about for a moment, and said, "Well, you're in for one hell of a sad story."

She said, sweetly, "Well, I have all the time in the world to listen to it."

I said, "Well, don't say I didn't warn you."

9

After breakfast, we'd spent a few hours going over the general "basics" of what had lead me to my life long bout with alcoholism.

I had begun with my earliest memory of my childhood, and by the time I had reached my teenage years, Catherine was in tears.

She said, "Oh my God, Chuck. How did you ever make it through?"

I lit a cigarette and said, "I don't know. I guess part of it was, I spent as much time as I could *away* from home, grew up on *street smarts* to survive. It has served me well – mostly, that is – except for the drinking."

She said, "So...was there ever a time you didn't drink? Any lucid moments?"

I said, jokingly, "Well, if you count the time I spent asleep, or passed out, I guess I did."

She said, "I was being serious, Chuck."

I said, "Unfortunately, so was I."

She said, "May I ask you a question without you being offended?"

I said, "Go ahead, it most likely isn't anything I haven't heard before."

She said, "Do you just *want* to die?"

I said, "Well, I guess I don't have much choice in the matter, do I?"

She said, "If you are referring to your cancer, you said you still had options."

I said, "Oh yeah, I could become a deformed circus freak that sucks his food through a straw."

She said, "Or, you could drink yourself to death. Not much of choice, is it?"

I said, sadly, "Well, it's the only two choices I have, isn't it?"

She said, "I have an idea."

I said, "I hope it is a *pleasant* idea. I'm getting sort of tired of the unpleasant ones."

She said, "How about a special dinner tonight?"

I said, "I have an even better idea. Why don't we have a little porch picnic this evening? Watch the sunset?"

She seemed to perk up at that idea, and said, "That sounds wonderful. What's on the menu?"

I said, "How about ham and cheese on rye, and cold beer?"

She said, "Can I have sun tea instead?"

I said, "Deal."

10

That afternoon, as we nibbled on our sandwiches and sipped our preferred drinks, I couldn't believe how beautiful the sunset was that day.

The way everything turned to a blinding gold and shined as if it were the only place on the earth. As if the sunset was meant for us alone.

Which was silly, of course. We had only known each other for several days.

But I kept the good mood going, and said, "That sunset is beautiful, isn't it?"

She said, "I don't think I've ever seen anything that beautiful. I can see why you enjoy sitting out here in the evenings."

I said, "Its one of the only things that's kept me sane, actually."

She said, "I can see why."

I said, "See? I'm not always a self loathing, pitiful drunk. Sometimes, I'm a happy drunk."

Shaking her head, she said, "That's not very amusing, Mr Chuck Polanski."

I said, sarcastically, "And I never professed to be a comedian, either, my dear. I'd always had alot of trouble finding a silver lining in every cloud, or a pot of gold at the end of every rainbow. In other words, I may have *read* fiction, or *watched* it on the screen, but, I didn't *live it*. I tried my best to remain in a virtual state of reality, no matter how hard times were to deal with. I guess I'm a no bullshit type of guy."

Sipping her tea, she said, "I can see that. But always remember one thing."

Sipping my lukewarm beer, I said, "Which is, pray tell?"

She said, "You can always create a *different* kind of reality for yourself."

I smiled and said, "Duly noted. Now, what shall we do for the rest of the evening? Other than digging into my psyche, that is."

She said, "Why don't we just play it by ear, and watch the sunset for now?"

I sipped my beer again and said, "I couldn't have come up with a better idea myself."

#

So, that's what we did, that is, until an old nightmare – in human form – by the name of Darrel Godfrey, dropped by for a visit.

That was his *first* mistake.

11

Darrel Godfrey was an asshole.

In all honesty, he was the *biggest* asshole in the entire Wabash County, Indiana.

If you looked the word "asshole" up in the Webster dictionary, it would have a picture of Darrel in there. If there was a poster boy for being an asshole, his face would be on the billboard.

Yes, Darrel was an asshole of the highest order, the King of assholes – the *President* of assholes.

He was an asshole when he was sober, but when he drank cheap wine, he became so obnoxious and intolerant, you wanted to punch him in the face.

Now, here he came, lumbering down the sidewalk like a pissed off bear, mumbling to himself and sipping from a fifth of Thunderbird wine.

When he glanced up to see us sitting on the front porch, he just couldn't resist being a smartass.

That was his *second* mistake.

When he saw us, he said to me, "Well, if it ain't the famous writer. I bought one of your books. I use the pages to wipe my ass."

Catherine whispered, "Who is that weirdo?"

Standing to my feet, I said, "Nobody to worry your pretty little head over. I'll handle it." I turned to Darrel and said, "Darrel, you have apparently forgotten what happened to you the last time you dropped by."

Darrel spit on the ground and said, "Yeah, well, you just got lucky, that's all. Speaking of getting lucky, who's the little sweet tart you got sitting there?"

Catherine spoke up and said, "I'd rather kiss a pig."

Doing my best to keep my composure, I said, "Darrel, you don't *even* want to go there."

Darrel said, "And if I do? What's going to happen, you old fart?"

I walked down the porch steps, balling my fists up, and said, "You *know* what's going to happen, Darrel. You'd best move on."

Then Darrel stepped closer, balling his fists up as well, and said, "Or what?"

"Or this," I said, and I gave him a hard right hook to the face. He yelped and went down hard, on his back, holding his face in his hands, as blood began pouring from his nose.

Looming over him with my fists balled up, I said, "Come on, tough guy. Get up, and face me like a man."

Darrel slowly stood to his feet, righted himself, and said, "Your girlfriend there needs a *real* man."

I said, "Wrong answer," and punched him again, breaking his orbital socket. He went down hard again, yelping like a wounded animal, and trying to sit up. I kicked him in the ribs this time, the audible sound of the bones breaking echoing off the nearby houses.

Catherine stood up then, and screamed, "Stop, Chuck! You're going to kill him!"

That's when the cops pulled around the corner, the cruiser slamming to an abrupt stop in front of the building, and a tall, burly cop holding a Glock 19 hopped ouut, pointed the gun at me, and said, "Stand back, sir. I think your buddy has had enough."

Lowering my bloody fists, I said, "Yeah, well, he's not the only one."

About that time, a familiar, dark colored Sedan pulled up out front, and my old buddy, Harlan Crow, the city Detective, climbed out, lighting a Lucky Strike non-filter and shaking his head in disbelief.

He knew me all too well, and knew that my temper had helped to fuel this current scenario. He stepped closer, took a long drag from his cigarette, exhaled, and said, "Well, what happened *this* time, pray tell?"

Before I could reply, Catherine was there beside me, saying, "That man was implying sexual innuendos toward me, and was acting in a threatening manner toward Chuck."

Crow looked down at Darrel and said, "Is that true, Darrel? Did you insult this nice lady?"

Darrel, still cradling his ribcage, said, "That's bullshit! They started it."

Catherine said, "And you are a *liar*, sir."

I said, "Don't call him *sir*, you're giving him too much credit."

Crow said to Darrel, "You need to stop drinking that cheap hooch, Darrel. It doesn't do much for your shining personality."

Darrel said, "Screw you, Crow. Just call me an ambulance."

I said, "You're lucky he's not calling a coroner wagon, you idiot."

The patrol officer said, "Well, detective? Is anyone going to jail or not?"

Crow said, "Not this time. Just radio for an ambulance for dumbass here, and I'll have a chat with mister Polanski."

As the officer radioed in for the EMTs, Crow pulled me to the side and said, "You're a lucky man too, you know."

I said, "Meaning?"

He said, "I could arrest you for aggravated assault."

I said, "How's that? He made the first move."

Crow said, "Yes, but he looks like he lost a boxing match with Mike Tyson. You could have punched him one time, and achieved the desired effect."

I said, "What are you saying, Crow? Just go on and spit it out."

Crow said, "In the future, you'd best watch your temper. I'll be retiring soon enough, and won't always be around to bail your ass out of trouble. Comprende?"

Swallowing my pride, I said, "I hear you loud and clear."

He said, "Good."

Then he turned to walk away without another word. Catherine walked over to me, grasped my hand gently and said, "What did he say?"

I said, "He told me I have to be a good boy."

She said, jokingly, "Do you think you can do it?"

I said, "I guess we'll see, won't we?"

12

Catherine and I had spent the rest of the evening sitting on the front porch, sipping our drinks and trying to calm down.

I could tell the whole mess had made her a nervous wreck, and I did feel guilty over that. But I sure as hell didn't feel guilty for defending her honor.

As we sat momentarily in silence, I noticed she was staring up at the stars above, her eyes partly closed, as though she was making a wish.

I said, "Penny for your thoughts?"

She said, "It's all so crazy, isn't it?"

I said, "What's so crazy?"

She said, "Isn't it obvious? One minute, we are sitting here enjoying a wonderful evening, and the next minute, you are beating the living daylights out of a man I've never seen before."

Feeling a little guilty again – but not much – I said, "Well, someone had to defend your honor."

She said, "I'm not totally defenseless, Chuck."

I said, "I wasn't insinuating that you were. But, you'll have to admit, the odds weren't exactly in your favor."

She said, "Fair enough. But in the future, please allow me to take care of myself, unless I request your assistance."

I said, "Fair enough. Now, what shall we do for the rest of the evening?"

Looking up at the sky again, she said, "Why don't we just sit here, relax, and make a wish?"

I said, "I think that's a wonderful idea."

But, I didn't tell her what I wished for; I didn't want to spoil my chance at a better life.

13

The next day, while my Queen lay upstairs getting some well deserved rest, I had retired to my laptop for a day of writing and relaxation.

That's the way I felt that day; like a Knight in shining armor that had rescued a damsel in distress, a Queen.

As I sat there typing away about my most recent exploits, my phone rang. The screen told me it was Kerry, my onocologist.

I took a deep breath, exhaled, and picked it up. "Yes, Kerry?"

She said, "How have you been doing?"

I said, truthfully, "Good days and bad days. Same old thing."

She said, "Have you given any more thought to our last conversation?"

I said, "Oh, believe me, it's on my mind on any given day."

She said, "And?"

I said, "And, I'll let you know my decision soon enough."

Then I hung up. I wasn't trying to be rude, but I wasn't in the mood for any conversations about the Big C that day.

#

Not that it would have mattered all that much.

A few minutes later, as I sat typing away, a pop up box appeared on my computer screen, that informed that I no longer had access to the internet.

Which also meant no access to my Microsoft word program.

No writing.

I called my internet provider to find out when my service might be restored, and the fella on the phone said it would most likely be around two days.

I thought, *Well...shit*.

Then the thought came to me; *I wonder if Catherine has the internet? I could use her service just for today, anyway.*

So I walked upstairs and knocked on her door.

#

Well, I *tapped* on her door – very lightly – and she must have been awake already, because she answered the door within a few seconds.

She was wearing a blue denim sundress and open toe sandals, and her hair was wet. I said, "Oops. Did I come at a bad time?"

She smiled and said, "You're fine, I was just putting on my morning face."

Her lack of makeup didn't make her any less attractive, but I didn't say so. I didn't want to think some dirty old man was flirting with her. I said, "Can I ask a favor of you?"

She smiled again and said, "That depends."

I said, "My internet is down for a couple of days.

Do you have internet service?"

She said, "I'm sorry, Chuck. The only service I have right now is for my phone. But I have an idea."

I said, "Such as?"

She said, "They have internet access at the college library, where I used to work. The public is allowed to use the computers too. All you have to do is apply for a library pass."

I said, "Is there a time limit on the computers? I have a lot to write."

She said, "Unfortunately, yes, but it would be better than nothing for now, right?"

I said, "Would you go with me? I'd feel sort of awkward otherwise."

She seemed to perk up at the suggestion, and said, "Sure. I could give you the so called grand tour."

I said, "Deal. I'll be waiting for you downstairs."

She said, "Give me ten minutes."

As I walked down the stairs, I had the strongest feeling I was going to enjoy the grand tour more than using their computers.

14

The college library was *huge*, so I was glad I had Catherine with me for the grand tour.

Wall to wall, desk top computers, as well as wall to wall students, most of which only served to remind me how old I really was, and how much youth had changed since I was a young man.

The clothing and the hair styles was caught my eye right off the bat.

As Catherine stood close by, chatting with her former employees at the reception desk, I had a few minutes to stand there and watch the spectacle unfold.

Some of the kids were dressed and groomed quite normally, while others seemed to have popped out of an episode of the Twilight Zone.

One young man in particular, a tall, bone-skinny guy with his hair shaved in a mohawk style, was clad from head to toe in bright, neon pink and green.

His hair – what was left of it – had been dyed pink, too, and he looked like he'd swallowed a pink hand grenade.

About that time Catherine was standing next to me, saying, "Things have changed a lot since we were young, huh?"

I said, "A little *too* much. So, what is the procedure for this morning?"

She said, "I already took care of it." She reached

into her purse and pulled out a small card with my name on it and a bar code. "All you have to do when you want to use a computer is have the lady at the front desk scan your card."

I looked at the card, and said, "Time limit?"

She said, "Two hours for the public."

I said, "Well, it's better than nothing. Would you recommend a desk top model for me? I'm used to a laptop."

She smiled and said, "They're the same as a laptop, just look different. You'll be fine."

As she walked away, back to the front desk to visit with her other lady friends, I walked into the computer commons to pick one out.

Like she said, they were all the same.

#

It hadn't taken me long to tire of sitting in the college library.

It wasn't just the kids, or some of them staring at me like the "old school dude" who had invaded their world, it was also the general *atmosphere* of the place.

This place was made for the young, not the old. I *was* an old school dude, and always would be, and would always be set in my ways.

So, about forty five minutes into my little visit, I'd told Catherine I was ready to go.

She just smiled, said she understood, and off we went back home.

She was always so sweet and understanding, I felt as though I didn't even deserve to be in her company.

15

But I always felt blessed to be in her presence, and would always feel that way.
Always.
Such a ...permanent sounding word, isn't it? Weird thing was, it didn't frighten me anymore, like it would have years ago.
Like the word...*love.*
Love is malice, and malice love. I have known this since I was a boy.
But Catherine is *different.*
I hope.

#

That night, as Catherine took a nap, I sat on the front porch, alone, sipping single malt and gazing up at the stars.
She had been right about one thing; at times like these, gazing up at God's creations in awe, it all seems so right, then, in an instant, it can all go crazy.
That's the moment I decided that I better enjoy life while I still had the chance to do so.
Before the Big C snuck up and bit me on the ass again.
Speaking of which, I had also made the difficult

decision not to take part in the radiation treatments.

If I *was* going to die, it would be on my *own* terms, not on Kerry's terms. I had appreciated her efforts on my behalf, but laying in a hospital bed with a face like a circus freak and suffering in pain twenty four hours a day didn't exactly sound like a thrill ride.

I hadn't informed Catherine of my decision yet, though. I didn't want to worry or disappoint her.

Just in case I was right about her being sort of sweet on me, like I was on her.

I hoped.

16

Early the next morning, as I sat at my laptop – my internet was back on! - I heard a light tapping at my door, and knew who it was. Only *she* tapped that way, lightly and quietly, gracefully.

I opened the door to see Catherine standing there holding a small cardboard box.

She said, "Good morning."

I said, "Same to you. What's in the box?"

She said, "I'll give you three guesses."

I said, "A lot of money?"

She said, "Don't I wish. Try again."

I said, "A motorcycle helmet?"

She said, "Why would I buy you a helmet? One guess left."

I said, "A birthday cake?"

She said, "You're not even trying. I'll just let the cat out of the bag, so to speak."

She set the box on the floor, opened the top, and I peeked inside to see a fluffy little black kitten lying on a soft bath towel she'd placed inside. It was sound asleep, but when I leaned in closer, it opened it's little green eyes and made the sweetest little sound, sort of a cross between a meow and a purr.

I said, "For me?"

She said, "Of course, for you. I thought you could use some company."

I said, jokingly, "Most bachelors prefer human company, that's all."

She said, "You don't like her? She's really sweet and friendly. How can you say no to that pretty little face?"

Looking down at the kitten again, I said, "Oh, believe me, it's nothing personal. But the last time I had a kitty, she died on me."

She said, "I get it. You're afraid of going through all of that heartache all over again."

I said, "Wouldn't you be?"

She said, "Yes, of course. But, this little girl needs someone. The lady at the shelter said this sweet little kitty has been sitting in a cage for ten weeks, and nobody has shown any interest in her. If she had stayed in there, she could have ended up being put to sleep."

I looked back down at the kitten again. It had a sort of *pleading* look in those green eyes, as if it was thinking, *Please, mister. I'll be a good girl, I promise. PLEASE don't send me back to the shelter.*

I could feel my heart aching for her, mister tough guy Chuck Polanski showing some true emotion, and I leaned down and picked her up and held her close to my heart, and said, "So, what should we name her?"

Catherine said, "That's up to you, it's your kitty cat."

Mulling it over, I said, "What's your middle name?"

She said, "Jean. Why?"

I said, "I think she looks like a Holly. How about Holly Jean?"

Catherine said, "I think that's a beautiful name."

I petted the kitten and said to her, "What do you

think? You like that name?"

She looked up at me with those big green eyes and made that cute little meowing purring sound again.

So then there were *two* special ladies in my life.

How could I not feel lucky?

17

Catherine gave me a ride to the local pet shop for a cat litter box, some cat litter, food, treats, and kitty toys.

We took Holly Jean with us, and she spent the entire ride propped up on her hind legs, on my lap, staring out of the car window, her face in the breeze.

To her, I'm sure it felt like *freedom*.

After we got back to my place, we spent the best part of the day getting acquainted with Holly Jean, and watching her play with her new cosmic catnip dill pickle. She seemed to love that toy more than the others, so I was sure I'd made a good choice.

Around dinner time, as we sat on the front porch watching the sun go down, with Holly Jean taking a cat nap on Catherine's lap, I said, "You were right, you know."

She said, "About what?"

I said, "About how crazy things can get in the blink of an eye. Just the other day, I was out here beating the shit out of a redneck, and tonight, I'm sitting here with my two favorite ladies."

She smiled and said, "Aw...you're so sweet, when you want to be, that is."

I said, "And just what does that mean, when I want to be?"

She said, jokingly, "I was just kidding, Chuck. Please don't get offensive."

I sipped my single malt and said, "Better watch it, woman. You're not too old to get spanked."

She giggled and said, "Neither are you, mister tough guy."

I said, "Why don't we talk about something other than ass whoopings?"

She said, "Such as?"

I said, "How about the fact that I like you and you like me? That would be a good place to start."

She cracked a grin and said, "Why, mister Polanski, are you saying you're sweet on me?"

I said, "And if I am?"

She said, "And if I'm sweet on you? What then?"

I said, "Then I guess that makes us sweethearts, doesn't it?"

Stroking Holly Jean's ears, she said, "I guess it does. But move slowly and carefully, mister Polanski. It's been a while since I had an admirer."

I said, "Fair enough."

She yawned and said, "My dear, I think I need a nap. Would you be too offended if I bid you farewell for now?"

I said, "To be honest? I'm feeling kinda tired myself. How about we meet back up at my place in the morning, for breakfast?"

She nudged Holly Jean awake, handed her off to me, and said, "It's a date."

Taking Holly Jean in my arms, I said, "Until tomorrow, my dear."

Turning to leave, she said, "Until tomorrow, my Knight in shining armor."

Then she was gone, up the stairs, my tired eyes trained on her until she was out of sight.

As I watched her go, I felt such a longing, one like I hadn't felt in a long time – that is, if I'd ever felt one at all.

I went inside and stood in my bedroom doorway, looking at that lonely place, amd how empty it seemed at the time.

I turned around and went into the living room, laid down on the couch with Holly Jean, and slept like a baby.

That is, until a demon came to visit me in the lonely midnight hour.

18

The demon alcohol, that is.

It knew I was *happy*, and had to give me it's personal opinion of the situation.

Get up, lazy butt! It's time for a drink. No rest for the wicked, you know. It said, in my mind. *Don't worry, Catherine will understand.*

"No, she won't," I said out loud, feeling a bit crazy for doing so. "She won't like it at all."

The little voice said, *So? You're a grown man, and a bachelor, too. There's no engagement ring on her finger yet.*

I said, "And there won't be one, if you don't leave me alone."

Then the voice stopped.

I rolled over and closed my eyes.

I didn't wake up until the next morning, when someone was pounding on my door.

#

It was Crow.

When I opened the door, he stood back and said, "Are you okay?"

Rubbing sleep from my eyes, I said, "Why shouldn't I be okay?"

Crow said, "You don't look hungover."

I said, "That's real funny. Why are you waking me up this early?"

He said, "Just wanted to warn you in person, Darrel Godfrey wants to sue you for assault and battery."

I said, "What the hell? You said I was in the clear on that."

He said, "Yes, you were, as far as me arresting you for it was concerned. But if a private citizen wants to file charges, they can do so."

I lit a cigarette and said, "So, what now?"

He said, "What now is, my Deputy will come by in the next several days, to serve you with a summons to appear in court."

I said, "And if I don't want to appear in court? What happens then?"

Crow said, "Then I would have no other recourse other than to issue a warrant for your arrest."

I said, "Please, tell me you're not serious."

He said, "Sorry, Polanksi. Like I said, I can only cover your ass for so long."

I said, "Fine. Is there any more bad news you want to tell me before I have my morning coffee?"

He said, "Nope, that covers it."

I said, "Good."

Then I slammed the door in his face, and poured myself some coffee – with a shot of single malt.

19

I must have experienced one of my blackout spells, because I woke up on the bathroom floor again, with Holly Jean snuggled up next to me, licking my face and purring her little heart out.

I reached up and stroked her fur and said, "You're so sweet, baby. Thank you for watching over me."

As though she understood me, she snuggled in even closer, and licked my face again. Here I was, lying on the floor in front of the toilet, a drunken mess, and my cat was there watching over me, making sure I was okay.

No judgement.

Just unconditional love and affection.

For a man who doesn't even seem to care if he lives or dies.

#

I eventually dragged myself up from the bathroom floor, gave Holly Jean some food and water, and jumped in the shower.

But not before voiding my stomach again.

Nausea seemed to be the name of the game these days, along with fatigue and pain and compounded with a bad hangover, didn't exactly spell success.

But I knew I had to hang in there, for better or

worse, or, in my case, until death do us part.

What an epitaph for someone's gravestone; *Here lies Charles Lee Polanski, who loved booze more than life itself.* The End.

I hadn't been laying on the couch more than an hour when there was that familiar tapping on the door. Too weak to answer it, I just said, "It's open."

I heard the old door creak open, then Catherine's voice. "Are you alright?"

As she stepped closer, I said, "I'll live. At least for now, anyway."

Sitting down on the edge of the couch, she said, "That's not very amusing."

I said, "It wasn't meant to be."

She said, "I heard your door slam earlier. I gather you didn't care much for your company."

I said, "It wasn't the company, it was what the company had to tell me."

She said, "So, who dropped by, if I may ask?"

I said, "It was Crow. He wanted to tell me that Darrel Godfrey wants to sue me for assault."

She said, "That's ridiculous! He started the whole thing. I'm a witness to that, too."

I said, "It doesn't make any difference. He has the legal right to sue me, and I don't have a scratch on me. It'll be a slam dunk case in court."

She said, "I'll go with you. As a witness."

I said, "I appreciate that. I'll need it."

She said, "I think what you need right now is a *break* from all of this. How about a porch picnic today, watch the sun go down?"

Holly Jean was there now, on Catherine's lap, and purring up a storm. Catherine said, "See? Holly Jean says that's a good idea."

I said, "Well, if Holly Jean says it's a good idea, then I do too. Let's do it."

Catherine said, "Around six pm?"

I said, "It's a date."

That's when she leaned in, and planted a gentle little kiss on my lips, and said, "It's a date."

Then she left without saying another word, out the door and up the stairs, light on her feet, like you'd think an angel would be.

Her lips tasted like peaches.

20

Later that day, as we sat on the front porch nibbling on deli sandwiches and watching Holly Jean playing with her catnip dill pickle toy, all seemed right again, *normal* again.

That is, until we received another unwanted guest.

I was sipping a cold beer and watching Holly Jean do a back flip with her toy when I suddenly heard the all too familiar sound of an ancient Ford pickup pulling around the corner near my building.

Darrel's half brother, Floyd.

As the ancient behemoth drove past my building, spewing black smoke into the air, it suddenly came to a bone jarring halt in front of the building, and Floyd rolled down his window and said, "Well, if it ain't the writer wanna-be and his sweetheart." He looked down at Holly Jean, grinned, and said, "You know, down in my neck of the woods, we *eat* cats if we run out of pigs or chickens."

Catherine leaned toward me and whispered, "Who is that goon?"

I said, "Don't worry about it, let me handle it." I turned back to Floyd and said, "You're liable to eat a bullet, you come near my cat."

Floyd smiled and said, "You know, if I'm not mistaken, that sounds like a death threat."

I said, "It wasn't a threat, hillbilly boy. It was a promise."

Floyd shut the truck engine down and said, "Yeah, just like when you promised to hurt my brother, so I guess you do keep your promises."

I said, "Your *half* brother had it coming, and I have witnesses."

Floyd's face furrowed into a frown, his eyes narrowed, and he said, "You don't have to have the same mama or papa to feel like blood brothers, asshole. I'd remember that, if I was you."

I said, "And if I were you, I'd remember what happened to your kin. You can leave now, unless you want to get hurt."

For a moment or two, Floyd looked as though he would bursting out of the driver's door and loaded for bear, then he must have thought the better of it, because he just leaned back in the seat and said, "Don't you worry, tough guy, I'll be back."

I said, "You'd best pack your lunch, then, because it will be an all day ass whooping."

With that, Floyd started the engine and pulled away, laughing and cackling all the way down the street, the truck's exhausts billowing black smoke up in the air like a forest fire.

Catherine said, "Well, he's just as unpleasant as his brother, that's for sure."

I said, "The whole family is unpleasant. I guess it's in their DNA."

She said, "Should I be worried?"

I said, "No. Don't worry your pretty little head about this at all. I've got it under control."

She said, "What about the court date? Do you

plan on attending it, or not?"

I said, "If I have no other choice, yes. But if I can figure out a way to avoid it, then I won't."

She looked confused and said, "And just how do you think you could avoid a court ordered appearance?"

I said, "You just leave that up to me."

She just shrugged her shoulders indifferently, and went back to sipping her tea and watching Holly Jean playing with her catnip dill pickle.

I, myself, sipped what was left of my beer, gazed up at the sunset, and made another wish, and hoped for the best.

21

The next day, as Catherine took another well deserved nap on my couch, I sat down at the laptop for what I had hoped would be a productive day.

I guess I should have known better.

As I sat typing away, I glanced up through the front window to see that someone had broken Catherine's windshield.

Trying my best to keep my composure, I picked up my cell phone and dialed Crow's number, and at the same time, hoping he'd already had his morning coffee. He was a real bear when he hadn't had his coffee yet.

He answered on the fourth ring, and said, "This better be good."

I said, "I don't know about good, but it's interesting. Someone busted my Catherine's windshield over night."

He said, "Let me guess; you have an idea who did it, too."

I said, "Do either of the terms "inbred hillbilly," or "dumb criminal" ring a bell?"

Crow said, "That could describe any number of kin in this neck of the woods. Are you referring to any particular family?"

I said, "Well, Floyd Godfrey dropped by here last night, acting and speaking *very* threatening. He even insinuated that he was interested in eating my cat."

Crow said, "Well, that could be taken as a genuine threat. He has been known to eat just about anything if he's hungry enough."

I said, "Yeah, well, he'll be a *dead* man, too."

Crow said, "Watch what you say, Polanksi. It can be used against you in a court of law."

I said, "I don't rightly give a damn about now."

Crow said, "Well, maybe this will improve your mood. The county Judge presiding over the Darrel Godfrey case tossed it out. You won't have to go to court after all."

I said, "You're shitting me."

Crow said, "I wouldn't shit you, you're my favorite turd."

I said, "I'm not sure if I should be flattered or offended."

Crow said, "Just lay low for now, and I'll take care of Floyd. And, try and stay *sober*. Alcohol isn't exactly good for your temperament."

I said, "I'll do my best."

Crow said, "Be *sure* you do."

Then he hung up.

So did I, and glanced over at Catherine, all cozied up on my couch with Holly Jean in her arms, purring up a storm. I hated to disturb them, even with good news, so I let them sleep.

Meanwhile, I had a glass of single malt and went back to working on my new story.

I was hoping it would have a happy ending.

22

Catherine and Holly Jean woke up around lunch time, to find me making grilled cheese sandwiches and tomato soup. I thought I'd give her at least one nice surprise before I told her about the windshield.

As we all sat at the table, with Catherine slurping her soup and Holly Jean sniffing her grilled cheese, Catherine said, "I had the weirdest dream last night."

I said, "What was it about?"

She said, "I'm not sure, really. I mean, I didn't really *see* anything in my dream, I just heard loud noises, like glass shattering."

I thought I might as well tell her about her car. I said, "That wasn't all a dream."

She said, "Excuse me?"

I said, "Somebody busted the windshield on your car last night."

Standing bolt upright out of her chair, Catherine said, "What?!"

I stood up too, and said, "Just calm down, dear. I have it under control."

She said, "I hope someone does! Because I sure as hell don't."

I said, "Do you have insurance?"

She said, "Yes, but I don't know if it would cover vandalism."

Trying to set her mind at ease, I said, "Oh, I

wouldn't worry, it should be covered. It wasn't your fault."

She said, "How am I supposed to get around for now? I can't afford to take a cab on my budget."

Before I could answer her, my cell phone rang. It was Kerry. I pushed the little icon and said, "Seriously, Kerry, this isn't a good time."

Catherine said, "Who is that?!"

Kerry said, "Oops, bad timing." and hung up.

I said to Catherine, "It was my onocologist."

Catherine's face softened a bit and she said, "Oops, sorry."

I said, "It's no big deal. I wasn't in the mood to speak to her, anyway."

She said, half jokingly, "So, what shall we do for the rest of the day? Take a hike?"

I forced a grin and said, "It would be better than sitting around here pissed off all day."

Sitting back down at the table, she said, "This is true."

I said, "So, how about we walk down to the corner market, grab something for dinner? While you call your insurance company, I'll cook."

She seemed to brighten up a bit then, and said, "It's a deal."

#

On the way down to the market, holding hands like a couple of teenagers, it couldn't have been a better day.

With the sun shining and the birds singing and two old farts like us looking forward to spending some quality time together, it couldn't have been more perfect.

That is, until we met up with Grandma Godfrey.

We were just exiting the market after making our purchases when lo and behold, there was his grandmother, Pearl, perched on an old lawn chair in the side lot, staring holes through me as we exited the store.

Without providing any explanation, I said to Catherine, "Just keep walking."

She said, "What's wrong?"

Then Pearl spoke up, her wicked witch toned voice grabbing Catherine's attention right away. She said, "Go ahead, Polanski. Tell her what's wrong."

I stopped, turned to face her, and said, "There's nothing wrong here, Pearl. Maybe you should go home, take a look in the mirror."

She cackled and said, "I was about to give you the same advice. But no, you couldn't handle seeing what an asshole you are."

I said, "It was a fair fight, and he started it."

Catherine said, "Yes, I was there, and it wasn't Chuck's fault."

Pearl said, "Girl, you must be as blind as you are apparently dumb. But I can't fault you for that, I heard that Polanski can be mighty charming when he wants to be."

I said, "Pearl, why don't you just go home, and change Darrel's diaper? Maybe tell him a bedtime story?"

Pearl stood up then, spit on the ground, and said, "*You* are the one that's going to need his diaper changed, when my boys get done with you."

Lighting a cigarette, I said, "Pearl, if I didn't know any better, I could swear you just made a death threat."

She said, "No threat, just a promise."

Flipping my cigarette down at her feet, I said, "I'll

keep that in mind as I beat your boys into a state of submission."

With that, I tugged on Catherine's arm and we walked away, with Pearl hurling obscenities at us in the background, until she voice was nothing more than a fading echo.

As we headed toward home, I had the sickening feeling that Pearl and her crazy family were just getting started.

23

Back at the apartment, as Catherine and Holly Jean relaxed on the couch, I took my cell phone out on the front porch with me to call Crow.

He picked up on the third ring and said, "Let me guess, you killed Floyd?"

I said, "Nope. If I'd killed Floyd, I'd feel a lot better right now."

Crow said, "Now what?"

I said, "Catherine and I took a walk to the market today, and ran into Pearl Godfrey."

Crow said, "That would definitely be enough to make your day unpleasant. Did she threaten you?"

I said, "Oh yeah. Said that her boys were going to take care of me real good."

Crow said, "Well, unfortunately, that's talk, and talk is cheap, in court."

I said, "So what do you suggest?"

Crow said, "We could file a restraining order on them, but they'd probably just wipe their ass on it and flush it down the toilet."

I said, "Great. Any *more* suggestions?"

Crow said, "Yes, just lay *low*, like I said, and let me handle it."

I said, "Great," and hung up.

#

When I came back inside, Catherine had Holly Jean cradled on her lap, playing with her dill pickle toy. Upon seeing me come in, Catherine said, "Well, are we still on for dinner?"

I said, "I didn't figure you'd be in the mood."

She said, "Well, a girl has to eat."

I said, "And a man has to drink."

She said, "Uh oh, one of those days, huh?"

I said, "I called Crow and he said the same thing, just to lay low and let him take care of it."

She said, "Which is something you don't want to do, right?"

Pouring a small glass of single malt, I said, "Each time I take his advice, my life takes a turn for the worse. Why should we feel like a prisoner just because Crow has to play it by the book?"

She said, "I know what you mean, but, if we don't play it by the book, you could end up in jail, or worse, if you get my drift."

Sipping my drink, I said, "So...we just sit here and lay low a little longer?"

She said, "And eat. Don't forget about our dinner you had planned. I think burritos sounds good."

I sat down on the couch next to them, and as Holly Jean nuzzled my leg and purred and Catherine grasped my hand gently in her own, I said, "How could I say no to my two favorite ladies?"

Then she gave me one of those good peachy kisses, and I felt a lot better.

24

The burritos were pretty good, but not nearly as good as those peachy kisses.

Then again, I wasn't really used to receiving any good kisses from anyone. Any kisses I had received as a child – which were rare and few – had always tasted or smelled like cheap booze or cigarette smoke.

So, Catherine's peachy kisses were a very special treat for me, indeed.

As we sat sipping coffee after dinner, I couldn't resist telling her how I felt about her kisses, and said, "Did you know that your kisses taste like peaches?"

She almost choked on her coffee and said, "Excuse me?"

I said, "You know, like the fruit."

She blushed and said, "I've never heard that before. But thank you."

I said, "You are very welcome, my dear."

She lit a cigarette and said, "So, what shall we do for the rest of the day?"

I grinned and said, "Why don't we sit on the couch, watch TV, and play kissy face like a couple of love struck teenagers?"

She grinned and said, "That sounds like fun. What do you think, Holly Jean?"

Holly Jean made that sweet little sound and snuggled even closer.

#

After dark, we all retired to the front porch.

After dark, unless I turned the porch light on, it was almost pitch black out there, so I didn't worry about anyone driving by and seeing us.

As we sat there, gazing up at the full moon and stars, I said, "So, have any of your wishes come true yet?"

She smiled and said, "Have any of your wishes come true?"

I said, "Uh uh. I asked you first."

She said, "Well, I'm sitting out here with you, holding hands under the moonlight, so I'd say yes. How about you?"

I said, "Ditto."

She said, "You stole that line from a movie, didn't you?"

I said, "I won't tell if you don't."

She squeezed my hand gently and said, "Your secret is safe with me."

Sitting on Cathrerine's lap, Holly Jean made that sweet little sound she makes again, like she was saying, *Hey, what about me?*

Cathrerine scratched her perky little ears and said, "Yes, sweety. You're included too."

We just sat there, gazing up at the night sky again, and after a few moments passed by, Catherine said, "May I ask you a question?"

Sipping a beer, I said, "Of course. Shoot."

She said, "What was it about me you found so special, anyway?"

I said, "What is there about you that's *not* special? I could go on forever on that subject."

She said, "I really appreciate the flattery, but could you be more specific?"

As I sat there, mulling it over in my mind, trying my best to come up with the *right* words to describe to her how I felt, I had realized there were *no* words I could come up with to describe it.

Sometimes, *actions* do speak louder than *words*.

I said, "To be honest? It's hard to describe my feelings for you in mere words. I know that sounds kinda corny, or maybe even like an excuse, but it's true. I'm sorry if that disappoints you."

She smiled and said, "Chuck, I would rather have an *honest* answer any day, than just a bunch of fancy words used to impress me."

I said, "So, my answer was satisfactory?"

Giving my hand a gentle little squeeze again, she said, "*Very* satisfactory."

I said, "Why don't we call it a night early? I'm pooped out."

She grinned and said, "More kissy face first?"

I said, "Your wish is my command, my Queen."

25

The next morning, as Catherine stood outside talking to the insurance lady about her car repair, I stood in the kitchen, smoking a cigarette, sipping single malt, and making scrambled eggs – but not necessarily in that order.

As I finished the eggs, I sat them to the side, placed a couple of pieces of bread into the toaster, sat down at the table, sipped my single malt – and then suddenly, everything went black.

#

When I woke up, I was lying in a hospital bed, hooked up a machine that made a funny puffing noise, and had a tube in each arm.

As my bleary eyes focused on my surroundings, I could see Catherine and a male doctor standing outside of my room, in the hallway, talking. He whispered something to her, she nodded her head in understanding, and he walked away.

She came back into the room, and upon seeing me awake, forced a smile and said, "Well, hello, sleepy head."

My throat hurt to speak, but I managed to say, "What happened?"

She sat down on the edge of the bed, and said,

"You were making breakfast and apparently passed out. You hit the floor pretty hard. You have a mild concussion and a few bruises."

I said, "I want to talk to the doctor."

She said, "Babe, you really need to rest right now."

I said, as politely as possible, "I *said*, I want to *talk* to the doctor."

She stood up, smiled, and said, "Okay, babe. I'll go find him."

While she was gone, I closed my eyes and imagined I was anywhere but in the hospital, hooked up to tubes and machines, but my day dream was interrupted by the sound of the doctor's voice. I opened my eyes, and said, "Yes?"

He said, "I said, I heard you wanted to speak with me, mister Polanski."

I cleared my throat and said, "I want to go home."

The doctor said, "That wouldn't be advisable right now, mister Polanski. You have a concussion, among other things."

I said, "Like what other things?"

The doctor said, "Mister Polanski, I have been chatting with your onocologist, and she believes that your drinking, smoking, poor diet, and your almost blatant refusal to explore optional cancer treatment is to blame for your current condition."

I said, "Regardless of whether she is correct or not in her assumptions, I still want to go home."

The doctor said, "May I speak frankly with you, mister Polanksi?"

I said, "Sure, as long as it doesn't take forever. I want out of here, today."

The doctor said, "Fair enough, I can't hold you here without a court order. But, please allow me to give you some friendly advice."

I said, "Go on, I'm listening."

He said, "You should stop drinking, smoking, and change your diet as soon as possible. Because if you don't, the next time you have one of your "dizzy spells," you might not wake up again."

I said, "Fine. Now, let's see those discharge papers. I'm ready to get the hell out of here."

26

Under protest, Catherine took me home in a taxi, got me situated on the couch, and began cleaning up my mess left over from breakfast.

As I lay there on the couch, petting Holly Jean, Catherine suddenly stopped what she was doing, stomped into the living room, and said, "You're one stubborn *ass*, you know that?"

Feigning ignorance, of course, I said, "Excuse me?"

She said, "You heard me, mister aspiring writer. How are you going to write a book if you're *dead*?"

I said, "I think you might be making too much out of this. I know this was my fault, but, I think I know my own body well enough right now to know what's good for me or not."

She stood over me, with her hands on her hips like a drill Sergeant, and said, "That's just an *excuse* to drink and smoke, and you know it."

She stomped back to the kitchen table, grabbed her purse, and said, "Now, Mister Chuck Polanski, if you think for a second that I'm going to stand by and watch another loved one die from cancer when they had an option, and wouldn't take it, you are sadly mistaken."

With that, she stomped over to the door, opened it, and said, "And don't bother knocking on my door any time soon, I need to be alone right now."

Then she slammed the door behind her – and on my heart.

Of course, I sat around the rest of the day getting drunk, to drown my sorrows.

27

Later that night, as I sat in the dark, sipping my liquid courage and chain smoking and hating my own guts, the self loathing was so strong, I had almost wanted to grab my .357 magnum from the closet, and eat a bullet.

As things turned out, I was glad I didn't, or there would have been *two* people dead that night.

#

As I sat at the table, just about ready to nod off, is when I heard the *screaming*.

It was coming from Catherine's apartment.

I don't think I ever moved that fast in my life, grabbing my gun and flying up those stairs. When I reached the second floor, I could see her door was ajar, and the lights were on, and could hear two people wrestling around and things breaking.

I burst through the door, knocking it loose from the hinges, to see Floyd Godfrey, with his hands wrapped around Catherine's throat, pinning her up against her table. Upon seeing me, she lunged out with her right foot and kicked him sqaure in the groin, and he went down hard on his knees, screaming himself now.

As Catherine stepped out of the way, I stepped in, and grabbed him by his shirt collar, pulling it tight around his throat, and placed the barrel of the .357

against the back of his head, and cocked the hammer back. I said, "You make one move, Floyd, and I swear I'll decorate this table with your brains."

Floyd said, "You don't have the guts."

I said, "There's only one way to find out, isn't there?"

Stepping closer, Catherine said, "Don't do it, Chuck, he isn't worth the bullet."

Twisting his head around to face me, I said to Floyd, "What do you think, asshole? Are you worth a bullet?"

Floyd said, defiantly, "Screw you."

Placing the barrel of the gun under his chin, I said, "Wrong answer."

Then I pulled the trigger – and the hollow clicking sound of the empty chamber made Floyd piss himself.

I smiled, looked at Catherine and said, "*Now* you can call the police."

28

While the EMTs were checking on Catherine, two uniformed officers were leading Floyd out of the building in handcuffs.

As I stood close by, having a smoke and enjoying the festivities, Crow pulled up, and as he climbed out of his Sedan, said to the officers, "I want leg shackles on him, too."

Floyd said, "I ain't no animal. Who do you think you're talking to, anyways?"

Crow said, "I think I'm talking to a piece of shit, but that's just *my* opinion."

"Mine too," I said, with a big grin, as the cops crammed Floyd and his swollen testicles into the back of a cruiser.

Crow walked over to me and said, "Well, at least you didn't shoot him before we could take him to jail."

I said, "Oh, believe me, I wanted to."

Crow said, "I bet you did. But, for once, you made the right choice."

I said, "So, what about his crazy half brother and his grandma? They won't take this lightly."

Crow said, "I already got you covered. Dumbass Darrel got himself arrested last night on multiple charges, including assault and battery. His granny tried to intervene, and got herself arrested, too."

I said, "Aw...that's a dirty shame."

Crow said, "Now that we finally have *them* out of the way, do you think you can behave yourself for more than a few weeks at a time?"

I said, jokingly, "I'll think about it."

Glancing toward Catherine, he said, "You best think about it long and hard, Polanski, or you're going to lose a good woman."

Taking a glance myself, watching the EMTs examine her throat, I said, "For once, Crow, I think you're right."

29

After the proverbial smoke had cleared, and it was just Catherine and I sitting on the porch steps, the world out there beyond the front porch seemed to stand still, like it was waiting for us to make the first move.

Or, waiting for *me* to do so, that is.

So I did.

As we sat there holding hands like a couple of love struck teenagers again, I said, "Well, this has been an interesting day, hasn't it?"

She took a deep breath and said, "If you could *call* it interesting. It was sort of terrifying for me."

Squeezing her hand a little tighter, I said, "I know, and I'm sorry."

Looking me directly in the eyes, she said, "Are you, Chuck? Are you sorry? If you hadn't been such a selfish, self destructive jerk, I wouldn't have been upstairs in my apartment, *alone*. If you hadn't shown up when you did, I'd most likely be *dead* now."

Before I could reply, she stood up, walked toward the front door of the building, and said, "You just think about that for a while, before you ever knock on my door again."

Then she was gone.

30

As much as I hated to admit it at the time, the first thing I'd thought of when she walked away was going inside, opening a fresh bottle of single malt, and getting drunker than a barrel full of retarded monkeys.

But believe it or not, I didn't do that.

Oh, believe me, I was tempted to do it. I did go inside, grabbed the bottle from the cabinet, and placed it on the table.

Then I sat down, lit a cigarette, and just sat there staring at the bottle like it was a portal into another dimension.

A dimension into *hell*.

I sat there for hours.

#

It was almost daylight when I woke up at the kitchen table.

I had fallen asleep staring at the bottle.

But I didn't open it.

It was at that moment I knew I could do this, for myself – and for Catherine.

I sat there for a few more minutes, then took a quick shower, and went upstairs.

#

When I knocked on her door, she opened it and flashed me a disinterested look, and, after taking a deep breath, said, "Yes?"

I said, "I have something to show you."

She rolled her eyes and said, "I bet this will be interesting."

I exposed my right hand, which had been behind my back, and she could see I was holding a full bottle of single malt. She said, "What are you going to show me? How fast you can drink the whole bottle?"

I said, proudly, "No." Then I walked past her, into the kitchen, uncapped the bottle, and poured every drop of it down the sink.

When I was finished, I said, "There. What do you think about that?"

She said, "I'll have to admit, it was impressive to see you pour out a whole bottle of liquor, but at the same time, *not* so impressive, considering the fact you most likely did it just to score some brownie points."

I said, "You've got to be kidding, right?"

She said, "Far from it. You have to *want* to stop drinking, Chuck. You have to do it for *yourself*. Not to make an impression on someone."

Feeling utterly defeated, I said, "So, where do we go from here?"

She said, "*We* don't go anywhere, at least not for now. You need to go back home, take care of yourself, take care of Holly Jean, and the next time you knock on my door, do it because you are *sincere*."

I was speechless.

My heart sank in my chest as I turned to walk toward the door. I stopped in the doorway and said, "So, see you later?"

"It's goodbye for now, Chuck," she said, and closed the door.

Of course, I went downstairs and opened a bottle I had stashed away.

Just for emergencies, you know.

Like a broken heart.

31

That day was the worst day in my life.

As I sat at the kitchen table, sipping single malt and chain smoking Luckies, with Holly Jean lying on the table, giving me the sad eyes, I almost broke down and began crying myself.

But, nope. I was *mister tough guy badass I don't need anyone* Chuck Polanski, whose self loathing is legendary, and whose courage lies at the bottom of a bottle.

Mister *dumbass* Chuck Polanski, who had the love of a good woman dumped right in his lap, and tossed it all away for the greater love of the bottle.

What else was new?

Not much, the little voice in my head told me. *Not much at all, dumbass.*

#

Over the next several weeks, I very rarely saw Catherine. I didn't even see her leave or check her mailbox.

It was like she had either vanished off the face of the Earth, or locked herself up in her apartment, had become a total recluse, a hermit.

Just like me.

#

About a week later, as I sat at the kitchen table drinking my breakfast and hating myself, I heard a commotion going on outside.

I walked to my living room window and looked out to see a police car, an ambulance, and Crow, standing there talking to the mailman.

Curious as to why Crow would be chatting with my mail carrier, I opened my front door to see two EMTs pushing a gurney into the downstairs hallway. Knowing there were only three other people that lived in the building – Mrs. Edwards, a retired school teacher, Mr Boyd, a war veteran, and Catherine – my heart sank in my chest.

Before I could even speak with the EMTs, Crow was there, in the hallway, saying to them, "It's okay, go on up. I'll be there in a minute."

As the EMTs followed his request, I said, "Please, Crow. Tell me it's not Catherine."

In one of the rare moments I'd ever seen Crow show any real emotion, he placed his hand on my shoulder, and said, "I'm so sorry, Polanski. Really I am. She seemed like a nice lady."

Blinking away tears, I cleared my throat and said, "How did it happen?"

Crow said, "The mailman had dropped by to deliver a package, and found her door hanging wide open. He knew she wouldn't leave her door open and unlocked, so he stepped inside to look around, and found her on the couch, already deceased."

I said, "What happened? Do you know yet?"

Crow said, "No official cause of death yet, no. But I'd say it might have been a heart attack, the way she was clutching her chest."

The tears flowing freely now, I said, "I hope she didn't suffer. I don't think I could take it if I thought she suffered."

Crow said, "Well, she's not in pain anymore. She's in a better place now."

I said, "You actually believe in Heaven, Crow?"

Crow said, "We all have to believe in *something*, Polanski. I would want to believe that my loved one was somewhere good, and healthy and happy now."

I said, "Yeah, well, I think my personal faith just took a nose dive."

Then I walked into my apartment and slammed the door behind me – slamming it shut on my life.

32

I didn't attend Catherine's funeral.

It wasn't because I didn't want to attend, it was because I was too loaded to attend. I didn't want to embarrass Catherine, tarnish her memory that way.

At the time, I'd thought it was the right thing to do, that is, until my landlord dropped by one day with the letter.

#

I had been sitting at the kitchen table, as usual, sipping single malt {It's good for you!} and chain smoking Luckies, when there was a knock at the door.

I half staggered over to the door, and yanked it open, to see Bill, my landlord, standing there, holding an envelope, with *my* name on it.

To Chuck

It was Catherine's handwriting.

I said, "Yes. Bill?"

Bill said, "I was upstairs, cleaning out Catherine's old apartment, and found this taped to the front of the refridgerator. I figured it was for you."

Taking the envelope from him, I said, "Thank

you, Bill, I appreciate it."

Bill said, "I'm really sorry, Chuck. Really I am."

I said, "Me too, Bill. Me too."

After Bill left, I sat back down at the table, poured myself another glass of single malt, and just sat there staring at the letter, as though I believed Catherine was going to pop out of there at any moment, and tell me it was all just a bad dream.

But that didn't happen.

After staring at the letter for a few more minutes, I picked it up and removed it from the envelope, my hands so shaky I dropped it twice.

After placing the letter flat on the table, I leaned over and began reading the last words ever written by Catherine Sanders.

Dear Chuck,

If you are reading this letter, I have either moved away or I'm dead. Either way, I guess we won't be seeing each other again, unless it's in a better place.

I know that sounds so wonderful, yet so lonely at th same time, but you know me; I am not one to mince words once I have something important to say.

Speaking of being a woman that doesn't mince words, I will just say what I have to say and get it over with, for better or worse, until death do us part and all that jazz.

To begin, please allow me to say I'm sorry for the way I acted toward you. I had no right to pass judgment on you, when I, myself, had been a problem drinker at one point in my life. I guess I was just scared that if we fell deeply in love, I would not only spend each day with a man who was slowly killing himself – just like my husband had done, with liver cancer – but I'd also spend each day being reminded of what a coward I'd been through it all, and a hypocrite, for passing judgment on you.

I guess my heart and soul couldn't take it, and I'd rather us part ways than make each other miserable.

I know to you, that may sound like a poor excuse for walking away, but it's all I have. I hope you understand, and I hope that someday, you really do find that one "special" lady out there, and live happily ever after.

With that thought in mind, I will bid you farewell – at least for now – and I hope you take your doctor up on her offer, and live a long happy life, and finish that book, too.

Love and hugs,
Catherine

I broke down in tears then, and, after bawling like a baby for awhile, I laid down for a nap.

As I slept, I dreamed of Catherine and her special peachy kisses.

33

My world was so dark without her.

The lonely days, the sleepness nights.

But the single malt was always there, to keep me company, to hold me in it's loving arms, to heal me from my wounds.

The *demon* alcohol.

I'd had more than my fair share of inner demons in my day, and all but the demon alcohol had forsaken me in my time of need.

It was my best friend, my constant, my lover and my enemy, all rolled into one.

She was the only friend I had left.

#

As the days turned into weeks, I wouldn't even answer my door or my phone.

I had officially given up on the world, and on myself.

All the while knowing now that Catherine must have known she had a heart condition, and even making the choice to run away hadn't saved her life in the end.

Leaving me *killed* her.

She should have just hung around for a while longer, and we could have died together.

#

But deep down, I never really believed that.

Deep down, in my cold, cold heart, a bright, warm, light was always trying to shine through, but I had always allowed my hatred and self loathing to get in the way, and extinguish that light as easily as someone would blow out a candle flame.

But one day, as I sat at the table sipping single malt and chain smoking Luckies and hating myself, there was a knock at my door, and for some reason I couldn't explain, I actually dragged my ignorant, self loathing ass over to the door to answer it.

It was Crow.

I said, "Good morning."

Crow glanced at his wristwatch and said, "It's the middle of the afternoon, by the way."

I said, "Who cares?"

Crow said, "Apparently you don't give a shit what *day* it is. You don't look so good, either."

I said, "I don't feel so good, either. Is there anything paticular you want to talk about? I'm busy trying to drink myself to death."

Crow just shook his head and said, "Now, that I can believe. What in the hell is your problem, anyway, Polanski?"

I said, "Why would you give a damn?"

Crow said, "I don't give a damn, actually. But I've always been curious as to why guys like you are so self destructive."

I said, "Guys like *me*?"

Crow said, "Yeah, you know, self pitying drunks

who are lucky enough to find *real love* for once in their miserable life, a *good* woman, and toss it down the crapper."

I lit a cigarette and said, "Why don't you just rub some salt in an open wound? I feel bad enough as it is."

Crow said, "Sometimes, a man needs to feel *real* pain, to open his eyes to the truth. Do you think Catherine would want you to sit around drinking yourself to death? *No.* She would want you to be happy, and move on."

I knew he was right but as usual, I played the tough guy. I said, "I'll deal with my pain in my own way, Crow. Is there anything else you have to say before I slam the door?"

Crow said, "Yeah, one thing. Why don't you go see your doctor again, before it's too late?"

I said, "It's already too late," and slammed the door in his face.

Then I sat back down at the table, closed my eyes, and day dreamed of those special kisses again.

34

I fell asleep at the table, and didn't wake up until my phone rang.

It was Kerry.

I answered and said, "Yes, Kerry?"

She said, "Long time, no hear. I had begun to think your cell phone had died on you."

I said, "Poor choice of words, Kerry. What can I do for you today?"

She said, "I was hoping I could do something for you."

I said, "Let me guess, you want me to go through a procedure that will turn me into a circus freak."

She used a different strategy on me next, and she said, "Fine, then. Just sit around your apartment and drink yourself to death."

I said, "Your bedside manner could use some work, doc."

She said, "And you could use an attitude adjustment."

I said, "That's true, but there is a method to my madness."

She said, "Yes, I heard your friend passed away, and I'm sorry. But that doesn't mean you have to do the same thing."

I said, "And just what is there that is so special to live for?"

She said, "Hmm...I don't know. How about your book? How about doing something nice in Catherine's memory? I could go on."

I sat there for a moment, thinking back on Crow's visit and now Kerry's phone call, and looked down to see Holly Jean sitting at my feet, with those big sad eyes, like she knew I was sick, and didn't want to live *her* life without me, either.

I said, reluctantly, "Okay, let's talk about it."

She said, "In my office this afternoon? Say about three o'clock?"

I said, reluctantly, "I'll be there."

For better or worse.

Until death do us part.

35

As it turned out, Kerry had been right about taking a chance.

About ten weeks later, after my first round of radiation treatments, there was no sign of any deformative side effects.

Other than some skin rash at the radiation site, some weakness and fatigue, and a sore throat, I was doing fine.

Then again, there was the task of getting that monkey off my back, the demon alcohol.

That task turned out to be the most challenging of my life, and my cancer seemed to pale in comparison.

#

But, after so many AA meetings, support from Crow and Kerry, and, of course, some of my own badass attitude tossed in for good measure, I managed to muddle through the process.

One night, as I sat on the front porch, in the dark, having a smoke and staring up at the stars, my mind suddenly drifted back to the first day I met Catherine.

There she was, still in my memory palace, where I knew she'd always be – and as though she had never left.

Those nice warm hugs and peachy kisses.

So, I light another cigarette and sip my sun tea, as my mind tells me, *Yes, Chuck. She'll always be there, and she will alwasys be in your heart, too.*

Make her proud. Stay sober.

Finish that book, too.

I close my eyes and make a wish on the stars in the night sky.

Suddenly, in my mind, she is there now, and she reaches over and grasps my hand gently in her own, gives it a little squeeze, winks at me, and whispers *I love you.*

I say, *I love you, too.*

At that moment, I realize that's all I will ever really need.

That, and Holly Jean, of course.

The *real* Catherine, a wonderful lady I know personally, who was the basis for the character of Catherine in my story. She is still alive and well, and still works at the college library.

David Boyer is a Christian, a multi-genre writer, a true crime buff, and the author of several coming of age novellas, numerous horror and scifi stories, as well as the author of numerous essays including the subjects of government corruption, Christianity, bullying, and cyber-stalking.

He lives in Vincennes, Indiana, with his cat, Holly Jean, who now serves as his copy editor by jumping on the computer keyboard when he's not looking.

Books: {Non-fiction}
True crime:
Small Town Murder: True Crime Stories From Knox County, Indiana
Murder In the Hoosier Heartland: Infamous Indiana Murderers & Fledgling Serial Killers
Murder & Mayhem In the Hoosier Heartland: Mysterious Disappearances & Bizarre Murders In Indiana
The Blitz: A Rape Victim's Story
Vanished In Vincennes: the Mysterious Disappearance and Death Of Dolores Oliver
47 Years of Hell: The Dolores Oliver Murder: Still Unsolved
Small Town Murder In Knox County, Indiana: Hate Crimes, Witch Hunts, and A Definitive List of Indiana Serial Killers
The Guy In The Blue Shirt

Non-fiction: {paranormal, bio & memoir}
Haunted Heartland: Haunted Hoosiers Tell Their Ghost Stories
Strange Happenings In the Hoosier Heartland
I Remember When, In Vincennes...Volume 1
Growing Up In Vincennes – Volumes 2 – 5
The Time of Our Lives: Growing Up Cool In Vincennes, Indiana

Essays:
Bullying: the Road to Recovery and Forgiveness
Privacy In the Age of the Internet: How Sexting and Sharing Private Photos Can lead To Cyber-Stalking
Once An Alcoholic, Always An Alcoholic? The Cold Hard Truth About Our Addictions
Travesties of Jutice: Flaws In Our Legal System That Imprison the Innocent
Will the REAL Christian Please Stand Up?
Racism in the 21st Century: ALL Lives Matter
Conflicted Souls: How the Man In Black Saved My Life
Crossing the Rainbow Bridge: Saying Goodbye To Our Beloved Pets

Books: {Fiction}
Mystery, Indiana
Human Sawdust
The Ghost In My Head
A Righteous Cop

Stories: {Long fiction, novellas}
Mystery, Indiana
The Mind of Luther Biggs

LUTHER
Jenny
Lester Talbot and His Magic Eye
Beautiful Ghosts
Pretty Flamingo
Jack and Norma Jean
The Things We Leave Behind – Volumes 1 – 3
Ghosts of Summer
Gardens
Claustrophobia
The Cemetery Artist
Brain Pie
Beast
The Jailhouse Movie Star
Easy Pickings
The Dominant Thumb
Joyride
The Maverick
Freak
Grandma's Gooseberry Pie
Dancing With the King
Always In My Heart
Hillbilly Moonshine Zombies
Home
Sheva
A Debt Repaid In Full
The Enlightening Darkness
The Good Neighbor
Wander
The Hungry Ones
A Gunfighter's Legacy
Dead Man's Hand
Inhuman Experiments – Part 1, 2, and 3

Jennifer
Spider Bait
Goodnight, My Love
Poor Larry
Creepy Crawl
The Ballad Of Georgie

Other recent book releases by David Boyer
{Now available on Lulu.com}

Dolores Oliver, fondly nick-named 'Lert' by her friends as a term of endearment, was out an out-going and friendly woman who was well liked by all who knew her.

Yet, on September 7, 1974, while on a visit to a local bar to chat with friends, she simply vanished without a trace. Foul play was immediately suspected by her family, who knew in their hearts that they could think of absolutely no one who would want to do her any harm.

Yet her lifeless body was found at the end of October in a bean field by a farmer in Illinois. Lawrence County coroner Dale Nichols was able to make a positive ID through dental records and a ring Mrs Oliver was wearing.

Who would have done such a thing, and why? Hopefully, VANISHED IN VINCENNES will help to finally solve one of the oldest cold cases in Indiana, and bring her family some closure they have sought for so long.

I Remember When, In Vincennes...

Hometown Stories From
Vincennes, Indiana - Volume 1

David Boyer

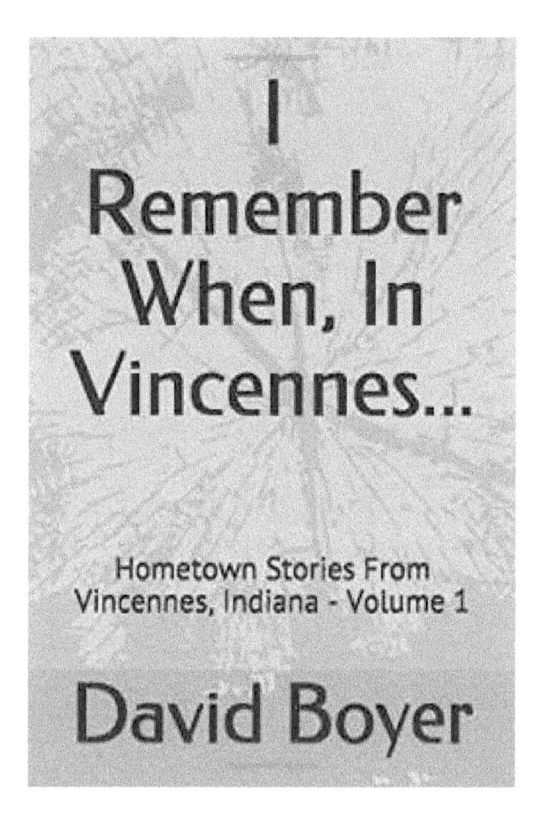

Unfortunately, even small towns – Vincennes included – eventually change, sometimes for the better, and other times, not so much. It's the natural order of things.

Trees grow old and fall. Sidewalks split and crack and are replaced for public safety's sake. Old houses – and all the memories associated with them – are demolished and replaced with parking lots or duplexes. Even historical landmarks, Mother Nature and Father Time having taken their toll, sadly, vanish – except for our own pictures and memories of them.

Luckily for Vincennes residents, local historian Norbert Brown has created a Facebook group page entitled, *Vincennes Remember When*, to help all of us keep our fond memories intact, and to reminisce and enjoy them 24-7.

It was his infinite wisdom of our local history and group page that was the inspiration for this book – and the stories within. Some of these stories may elicit a tear, some laughter.

Some may remind you of an old friend you haven't seen since high school – or, sadly, one that has passed in recent years. Some may remind you of your childhood, your teenage years – or having to bid them farewell, in order to move on to bigger and better things; marriage, children, grandchildren, and a lifetime of wonderful memories that only a tight-knit, loving family can provide.

It is my sincere belief that there will be a story for *everybody* within these pages, regardless of whether you may be a Vincennes history buff or not.

Small Town Murder In Knox County, Indiana

Hate Crimes, Witch Hunts, and A Definitive List Of Indiana Serial Killers

David Boyer

As of 2015, it is believed that there are at least 200 serial killers active in the United States at any given time.

33 of them were from Indiana.

Nobody in their own home town would have wanted to imagine a fledgling {or full fledged} serial killer lurking about, searching for his next victim. Or imagine one being their next door neighbor or the relative of a friend or even attending the local college.

Yet, since the early 1970s, Vincennes, Indiana, Knox County, and Indiana in general has had it's share of cold blooded murder.

It's really sad – as well as terrifying – to even

imagine all these brutal, cold blooded murders have taken place in small town communities, where, at one time, we could all trust just about everyone we met at least to the extent they'd do us no harm; a time when could leave our doors unlocked at night or a window open for a cool breeze or not have to worry about where our children were – or if they'd ever come home again.

In SMALL TOWN MURDER, we will be examining local cases, old cases, more recent cases, and the aftermath it leaves behind for the victim's families – as well as taking an in-depth look into a deep, dark, world none of us would ever want to see – but has been here all along, and, most likely, always will be.